Face TO Face
with the Easter Bunny
a TJ Gram Interview
Illustrations by Jessica Gamboa
I0746293

Copyright 2024

Dedication

To Dane, Macy, and Meg. What truly amazing
parents you are, and how lucky I am to be
one of yours.

Acknowledgment

For Rhaymond, Bryce, and Rhett and all of my former students. It was an honor being your teacher.

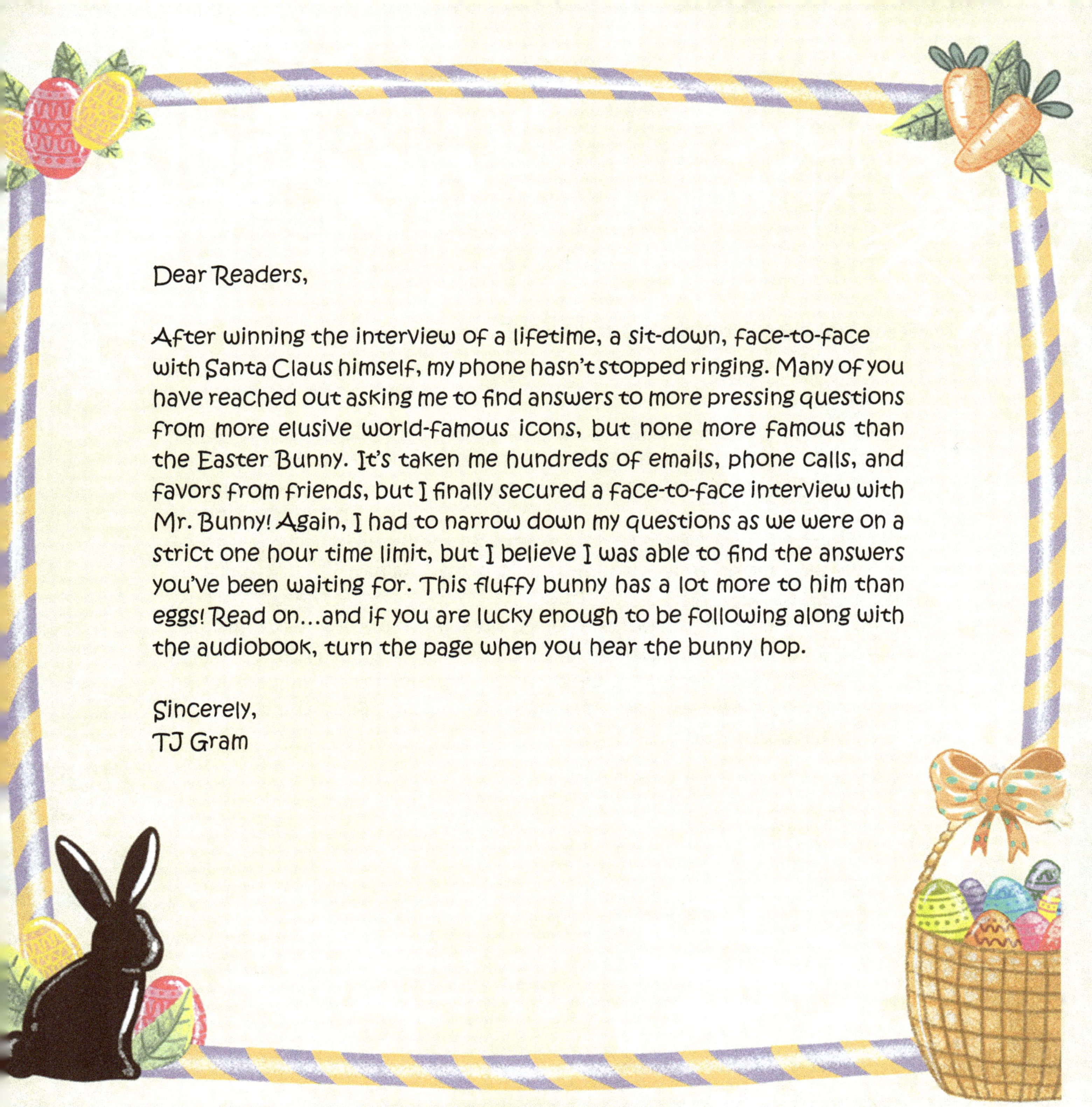

Dear Readers,

After winning the interview of a lifetime, a sit-down, face-to-face with Santa Claus himself, my phone hasn't stopped ringing. Many of you have reached out asking me to find answers to more pressing questions from more elusive world-famous icons, but none more famous than the Easter Bunny. It's taken me hundreds of emails, phone calls, and favors from friends, but I finally secured a face-to-face interview with Mr. Bunny! Again, I had to narrow down my questions as we were on a strict one hour time limit, but I believe I was able to find the answers you've been waiting for. This fluffy bunny has a lot more to him than eggs! Read on...and if you are lucky enough to be following along with the audiobook, turn the page when you hear the bunny hop.

Sincerely,
TJ Gram

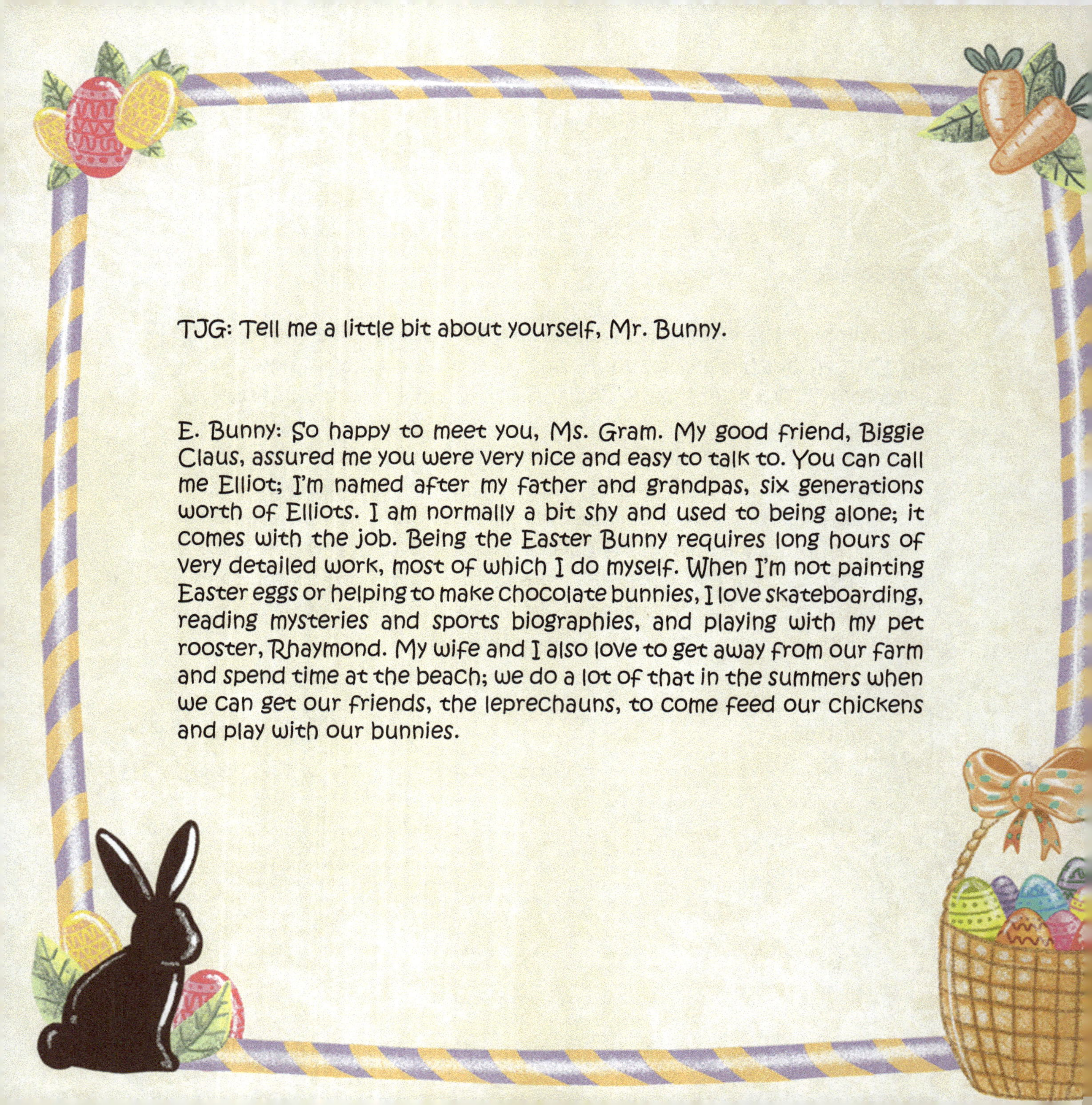

TJG: Tell me a little bit about yourself, Mr. Bunny.

E. Bunny: So happy to meet you, Ms. Gram. My good friend, Biggie Claus, assured me you were very nice and easy to talk to. You can call me Elliot; I'm named after my father and grandpas, six generations worth of Elliots. I am normally a bit shy and used to being alone; it comes with the job. Being the Easter Bunny requires long hours of very detailed work, most of which I do myself. When I'm not painting Easter eggs or helping to make chocolate bunnies, I love skateboarding, reading mysteries and sports biographies, and playing with my pet rooster, Rhaymond. My wife and I also love to get away from our farm and spend time at the beach; we do a lot of that in the summers when we can get our friends, the leprechauns, to come feed our chickens and play with our bunnies.

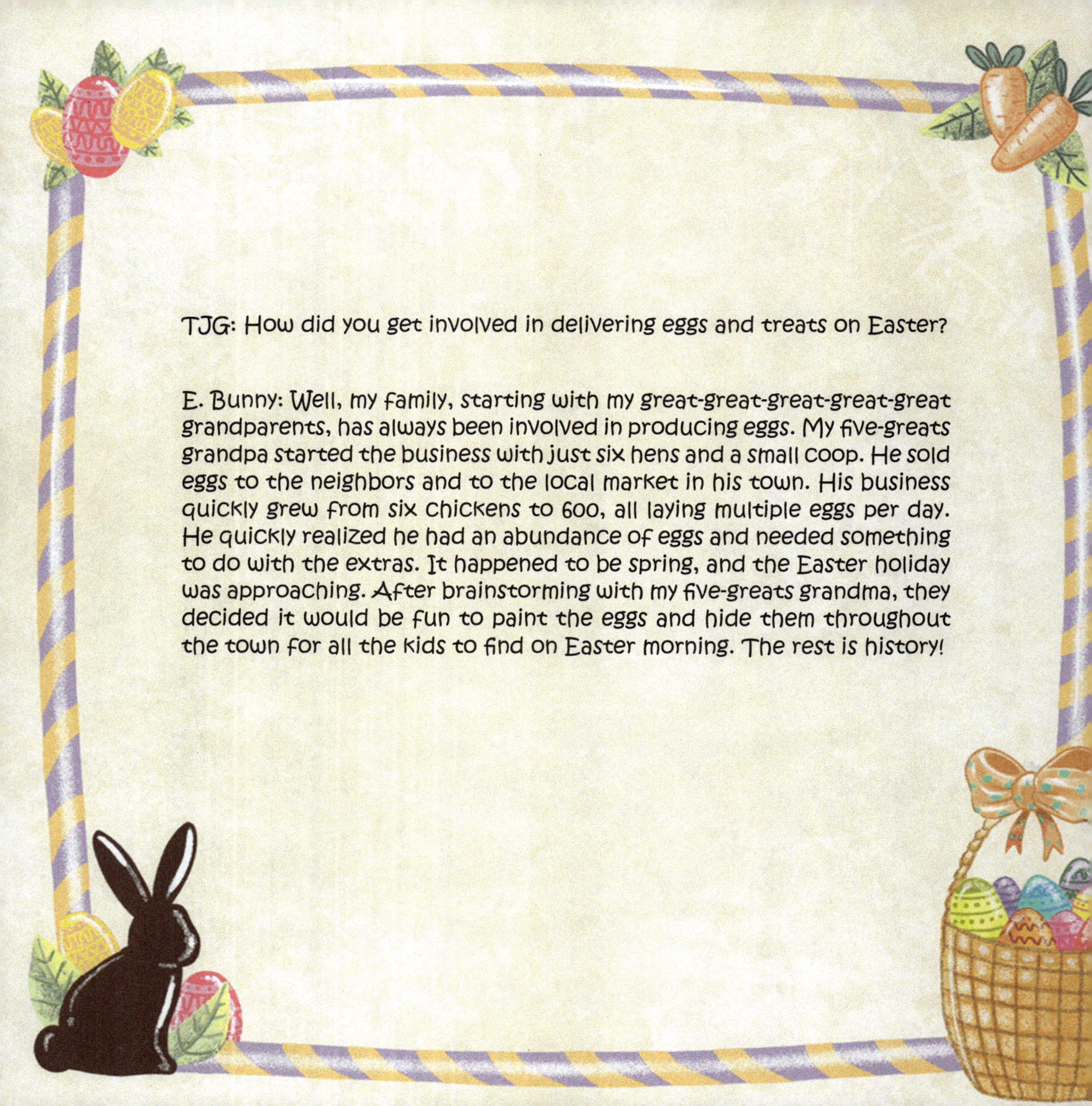

TJG: How did you get involved in delivering eggs and treats on Easter?

E. Bunny: Well, my family, starting with my great-great-great-great-great grandparents, has always been involved in producing eggs. My five-greats grandpa started the business with just six hens and a small coop. He sold eggs to the neighbors and to the local market in his town. His business quickly grew from six chickens to 600, all laying multiple eggs per day. He quickly realized he had an abundance of eggs and needed something to do with the extras. It happened to be spring, and the Easter holiday was approaching. After brainstorming with my five-greats grandma, they decided it would be fun to paint the eggs and hide them throughout the town for all the kids to find on Easter morning. The rest is history!

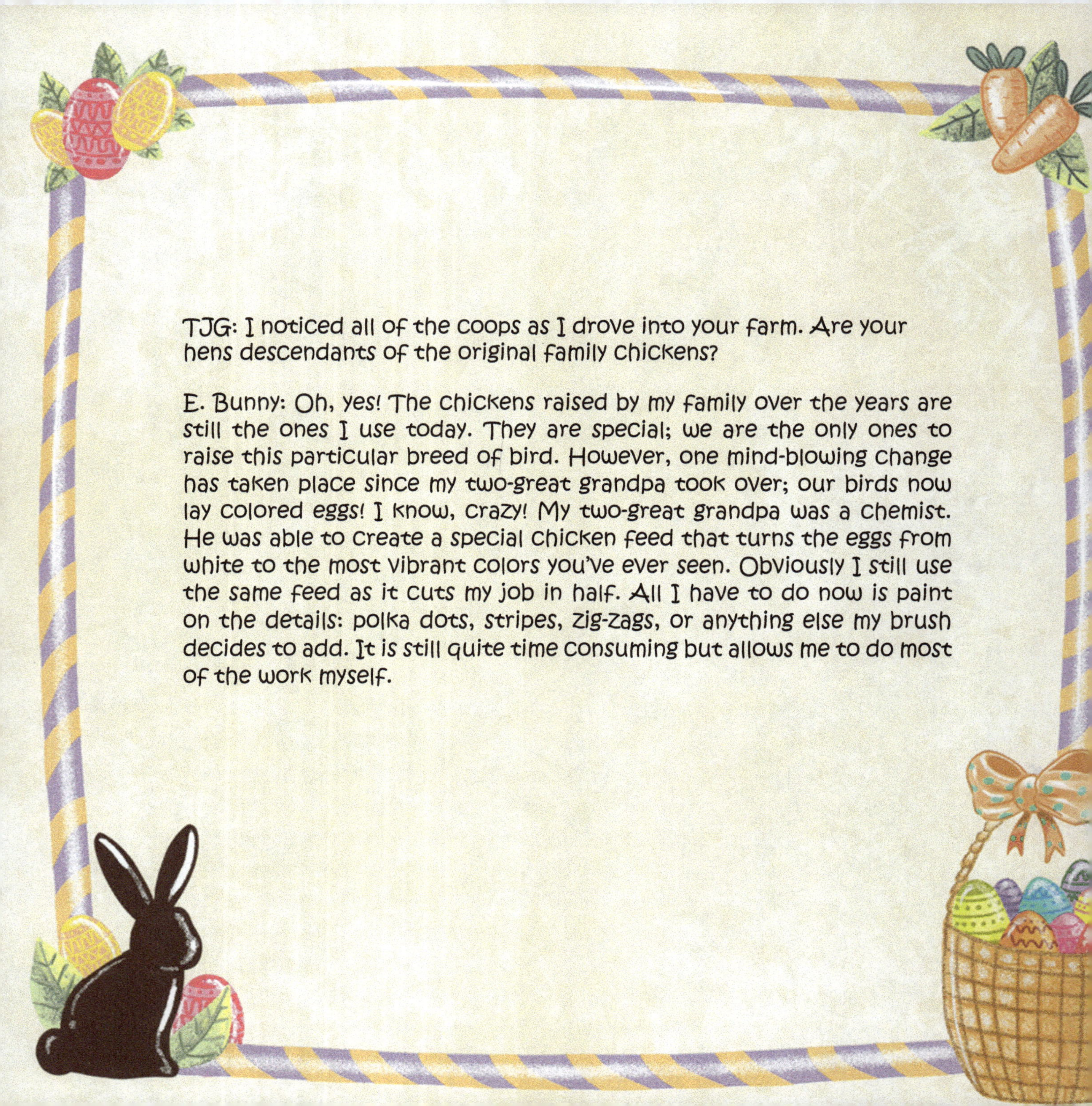

TJG: I noticed all of the coops as I drove into your farm. Are your hens descendants of the original family chickens?

E. Bunny: Oh, yes! The chickens raised by my family over the years are still the ones I use today. They are special; we are the only ones to raise this particular breed of bird. However, one mind-blowing change has taken place since my two-great grandpa took over; our birds now lay colored eggs! I know, crazy! My two-great grandpa was a chemist. He was able to create a special chicken feed that turns the eggs from white to the most vibrant colors you've ever seen. Obviously I still use the same feed as it cuts my job in half. All I have to do now is paint on the details: polka dots, stripes, zig-zags, or anything else my brush decides to add. It is still quite time consuming but allows me to do most of the work myself.

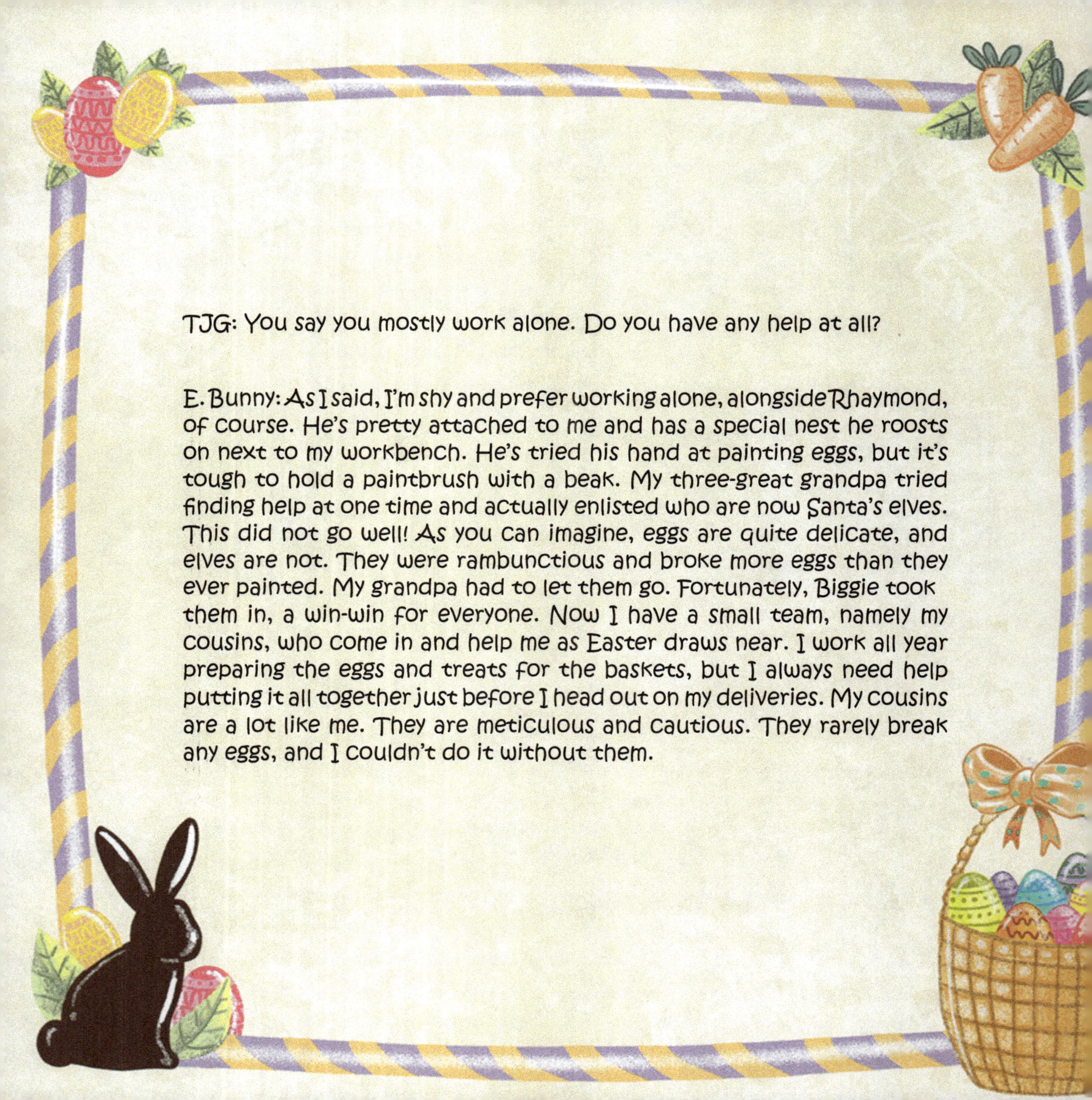

TJG: You say you mostly work alone. Do you have any help at all?

E. Bunny: As I said, I'm shy and prefer working alone, alongside Rhaymond, of course. He's pretty attached to me and has a special nest he roosts on next to my workbench. He's tried his hand at painting eggs, but it's tough to hold a paintbrush with a beak. My three-great grandpa tried finding help at one time and actually enlisted who are now Santa's elves. This did not go well! As you can imagine, eggs are quite delicate, and elves are not. They were rambunctious and broke more eggs than they ever painted. My grandpa had to let them go. Fortunately, Biggie took them in, a win-win for everyone. Now I have a small team, namely my cousins, who come in and help me as Easter draws near. I work all year preparing the eggs and treats for the baskets, but I always need help putting it all together just before I head out on my deliveries. My cousins are a lot like me. They are meticulous and cautious. They rarely break any eggs, and I couldn't do it without them.

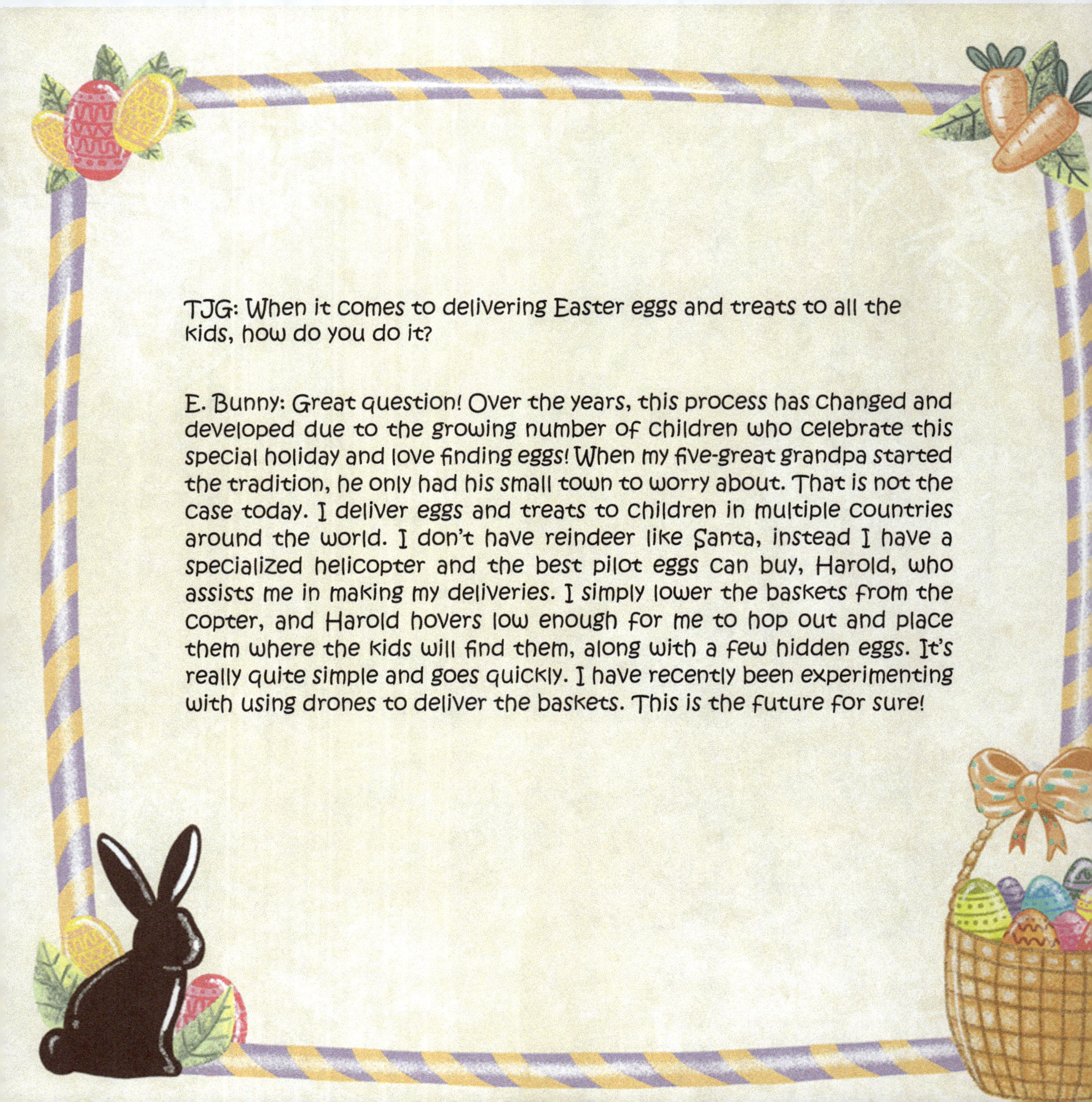

TJG: When it comes to delivering Easter eggs and treats to all the kids, how do you do it?

E. Bunny: Great question! Over the years, this process has changed and developed due to the growing number of children who celebrate this special holiday and love finding eggs! When my five-great grandpa started the tradition, he only had his small town to worry about. That is not the case today. I deliver eggs and treats to children in multiple countries around the world. I don't have reindeer like Santa, instead I have a specialized helicopter and the best pilot eggs can buy, Harold, who assists me in making my deliveries. I simply lower the baskets from the copter, and Harold hovers low enough for me to hop out and place them where the kids will find them, along with a few hidden eggs. It's really quite simple and goes quickly. I have recently been experimenting with using drones to deliver the baskets. This is the future for sure!

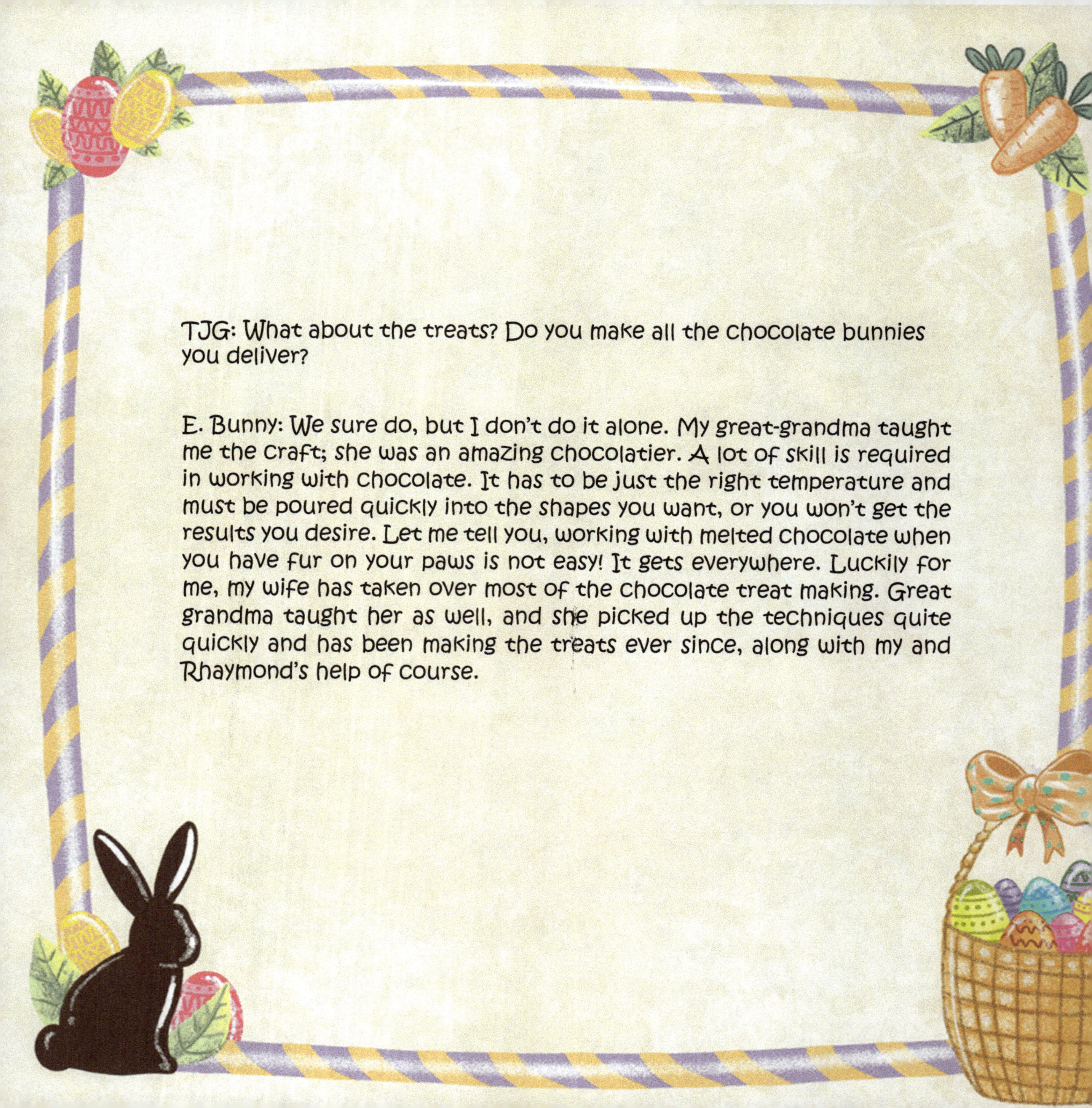

TJG: What about the treats? Do you make all the chocolate bunnies you deliver?

E. Bunny: We sure do, but I don't do it alone. My great-grandma taught me the craft; she was an amazing chocolatier. A lot of skill is required in working with chocolate. It has to be just the right temperature and must be poured quickly into the shapes you want, or you won't get the results you desire. Let me tell you, working with melted chocolate when you have fur on your paws is not easy! It gets everywhere. Luckily for me, my wife has taken over most of the chocolate treat making. Great grandma taught her as well, and she picked up the techniques quite quickly and has been making the treats ever since, along with my and Rhaymond's help of course.

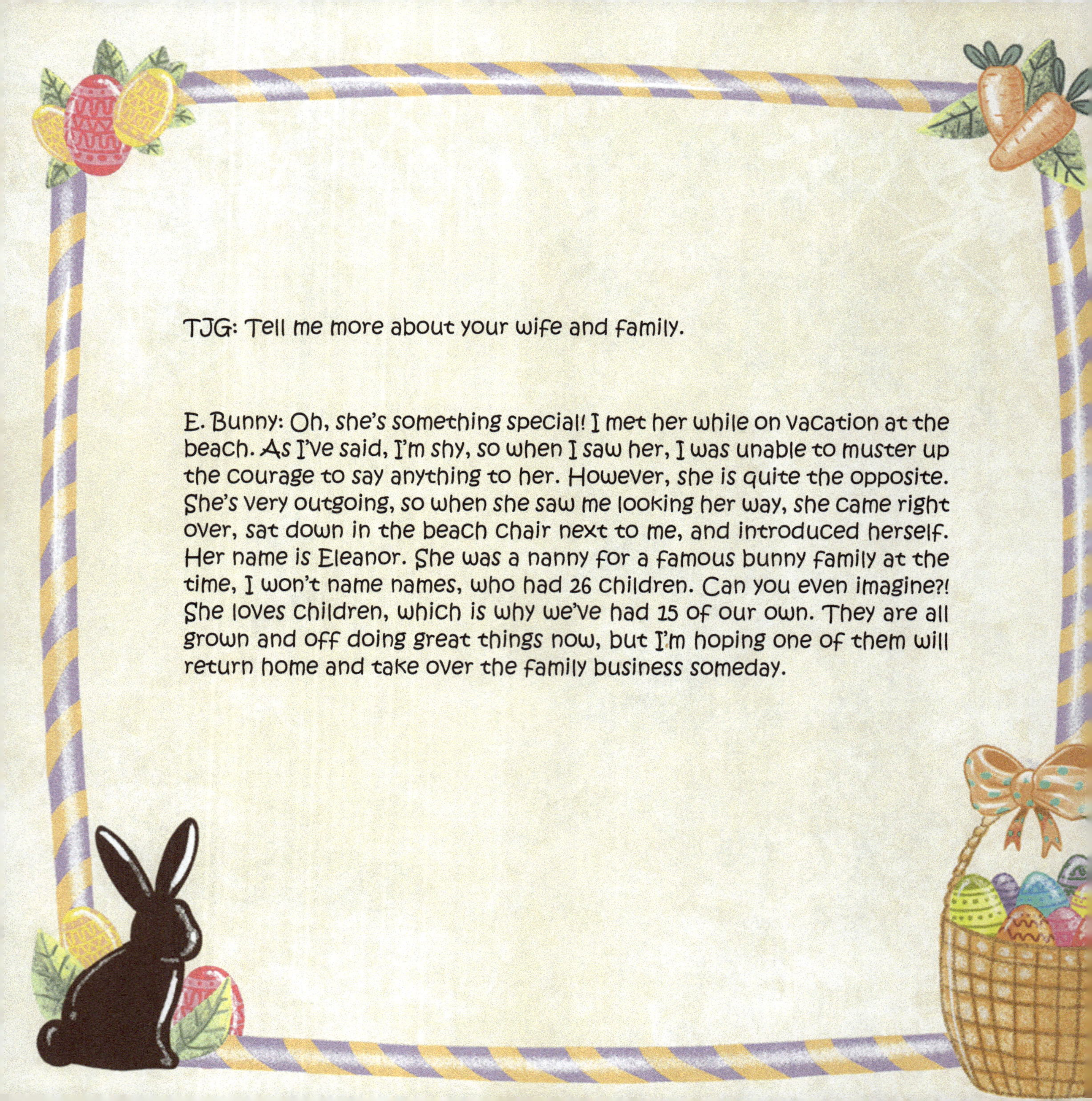

TJG: Tell me more about your wife and family.

E. Bunny: Oh, she's something special! I met her while on vacation at the beach. As I've said, I'm shy, so when I saw her, I was unable to muster up the courage to say anything to her. However, she is quite the opposite. She's very outgoing, so when she saw me looking her way, she came right over, sat down in the beach chair next to me, and introduced herself. Her name is Eleanor. She was a nanny for a famous bunny family at the time, I won't name names, who had 26 children. Can you even imagine?! She loves children, which is why we've had 15 of our own. They are all grown and off doing great things now, but I'm hoping one of them will return home and take over the family business someday.

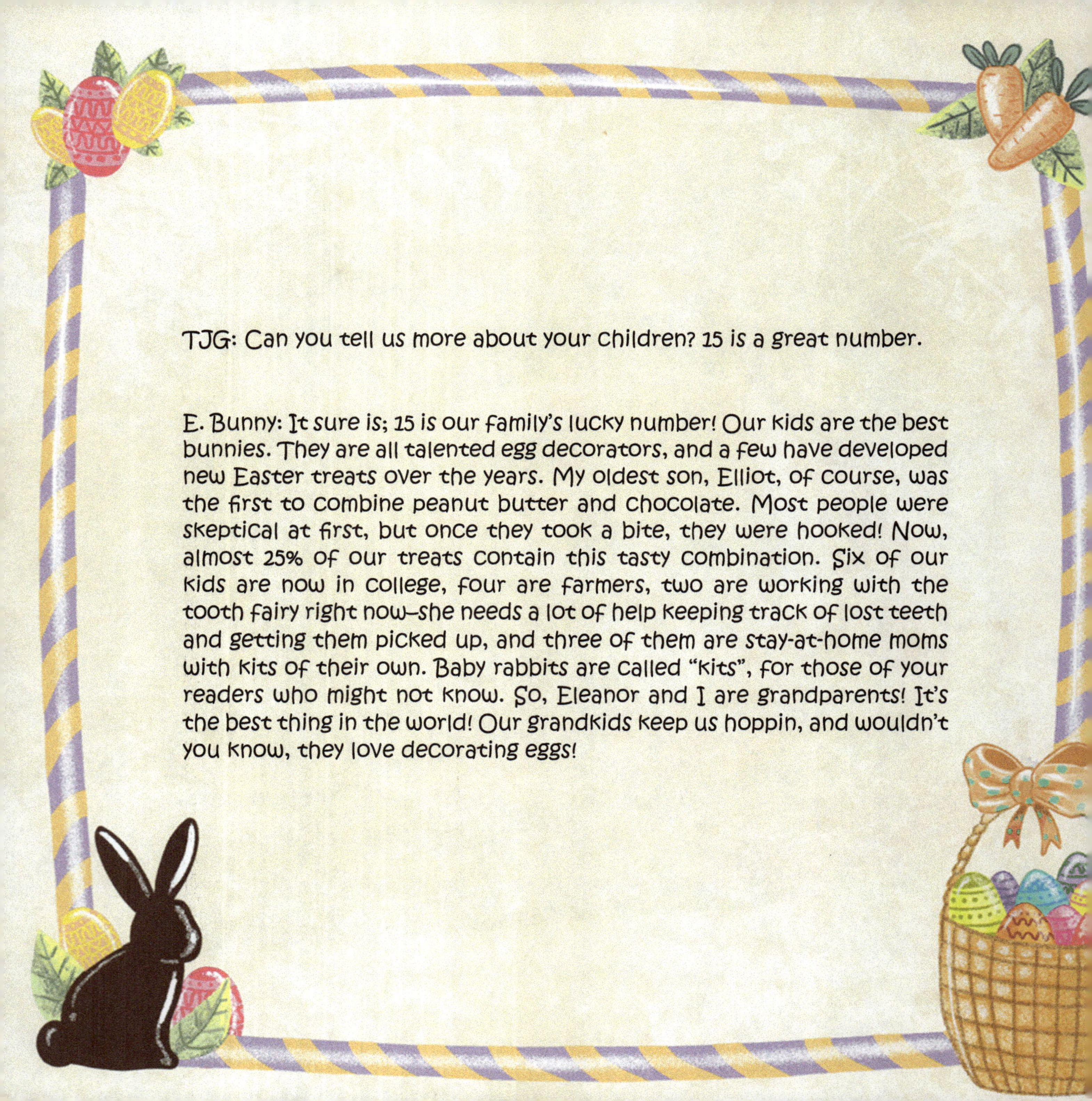

TJG: Can you tell us more about your children? 15 is a great number.

E. Bunny: It sure is; 15 is our family's lucky number! Our kids are the best bunnies. They are all talented egg decorators, and a few have developed new Easter treats over the years. My oldest son, Elliot, of course, was the first to combine peanut butter and chocolate. Most people were skeptical at first, but once they took a bite, they were hooked! Now, almost 25% of our treats contain this tasty combination. Six of our kids are now in college, four are farmers, two are working with the tooth fairy right now—she needs a lot of help keeping track of lost teeth and getting them picked up, and three of them are stay-at-home moms with kits of their own. Baby rabbits are called "kits", for those of your readers who might not know. So, Eleanor and I are grandparents! It's the best thing in the world! Our grandkids keep us hoppin, and wouldn't you know, they love decorating eggs!

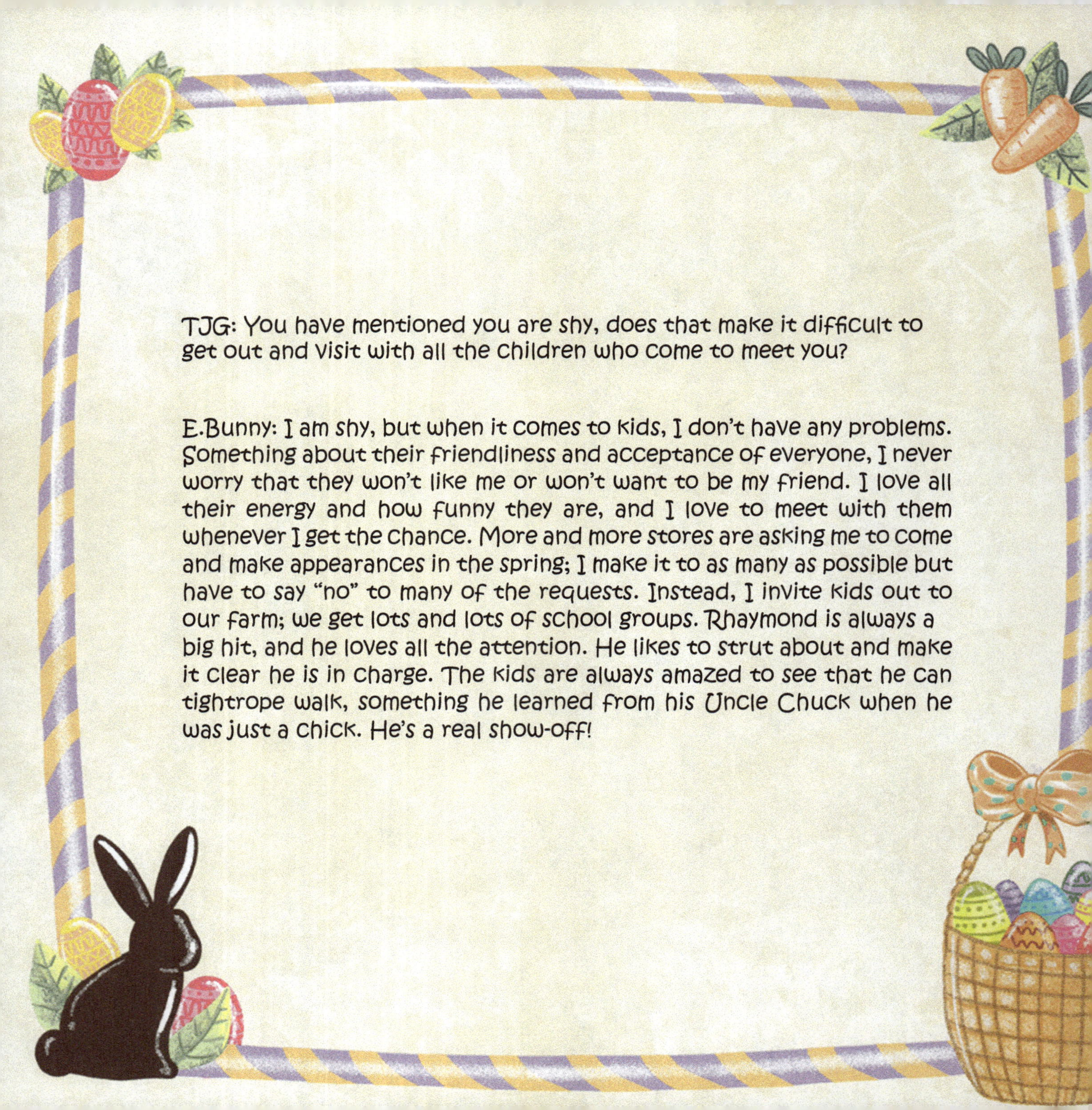

TJG: You have mentioned you are shy, does that make it difficult to get out and visit with all the children who come to meet you?

E.Bunny: I am shy, but when it comes to kids, I don't have any problems. Something about their friendliness and acceptance of everyone, I never worry that they won't like me or won't want to be my friend. I love all their energy and how funny they are, and I love to meet with them whenever I get the chance. More and more stores are asking me to come and make appearances in the spring; I make it to as many as possible but have to say "no" to many of the requests. Instead, I invite kids out to our farm; we get lots and lots of school groups. Rhaymond is always a big hit, and he loves all the attention. He likes to strut about and make it clear he is in charge. The kids are always amazed to see that he can tightrope walk, something he learned from his Uncle Chuck when he was just a chick. He's a real show-off!

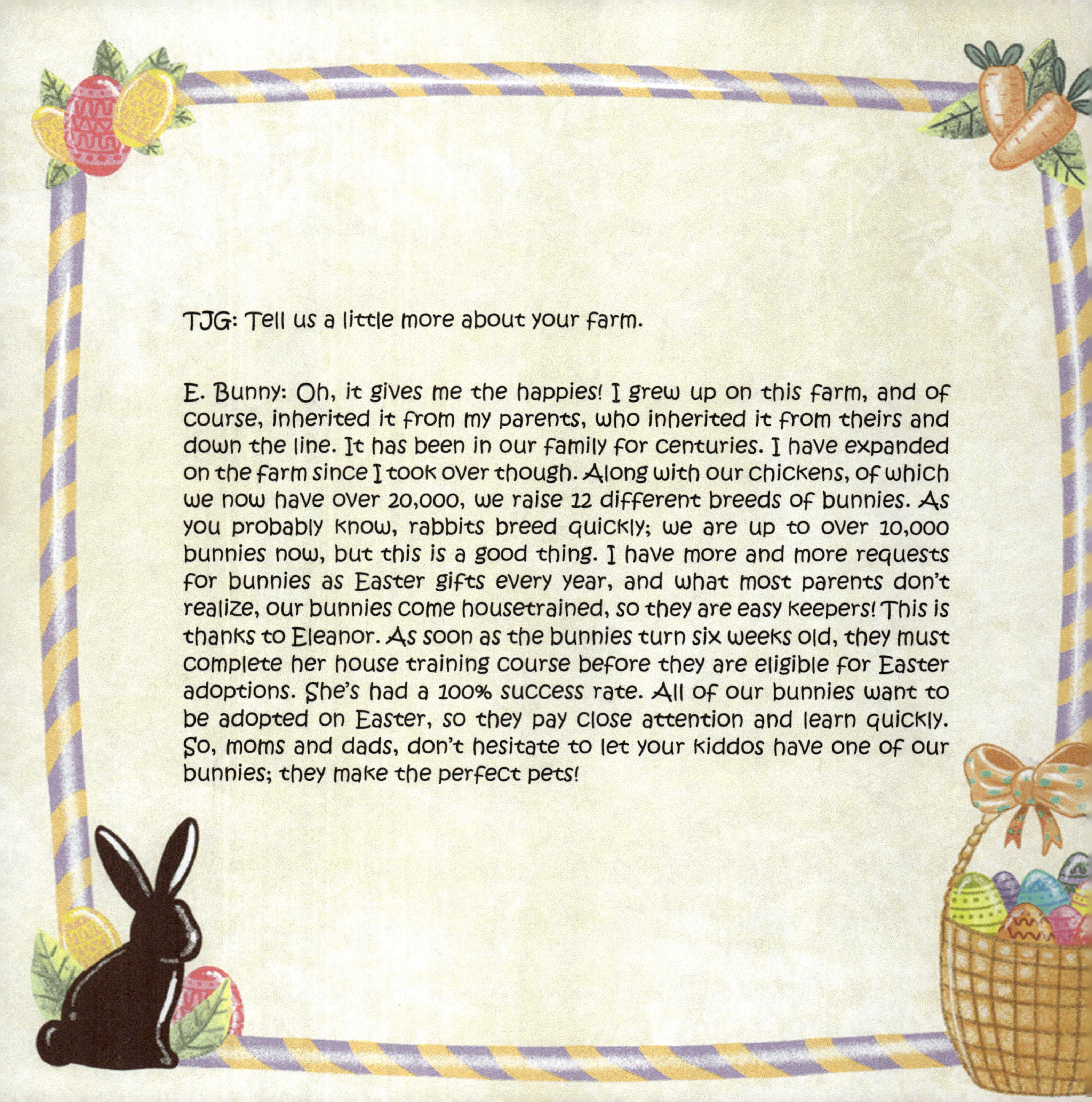

TJG: Tell us a little more about your farm.

E. Bunny: Oh, it gives me the happies! I grew up on this farm, and of course, inherited it from my parents, who inherited it from theirs and down the line. It has been in our family for centuries. I have expanded on the farm since I took over though. Along with our chickens, of which we now have over 20,000, we raise 12 different breeds of bunnies. As you probably know, rabbits breed quickly; we are up to over 10,000 bunnies now, but this is a good thing. I have more and more requests for bunnies as Easter gifts every year, and what most parents don't realize, our bunnies come housetrained, so they are easy keepers! This is thanks to Eleanor. As soon as the bunnies turn six weeks old, they must complete her house training course before they are eligible for Easter adoptions. She's had a 100% success rate. All of our bunnies want to be adopted on Easter, so they pay close attention and learn quickly. So, moms and dads, don't hesitate to let your kiddos have one of our bunnies; they make the perfect pets!

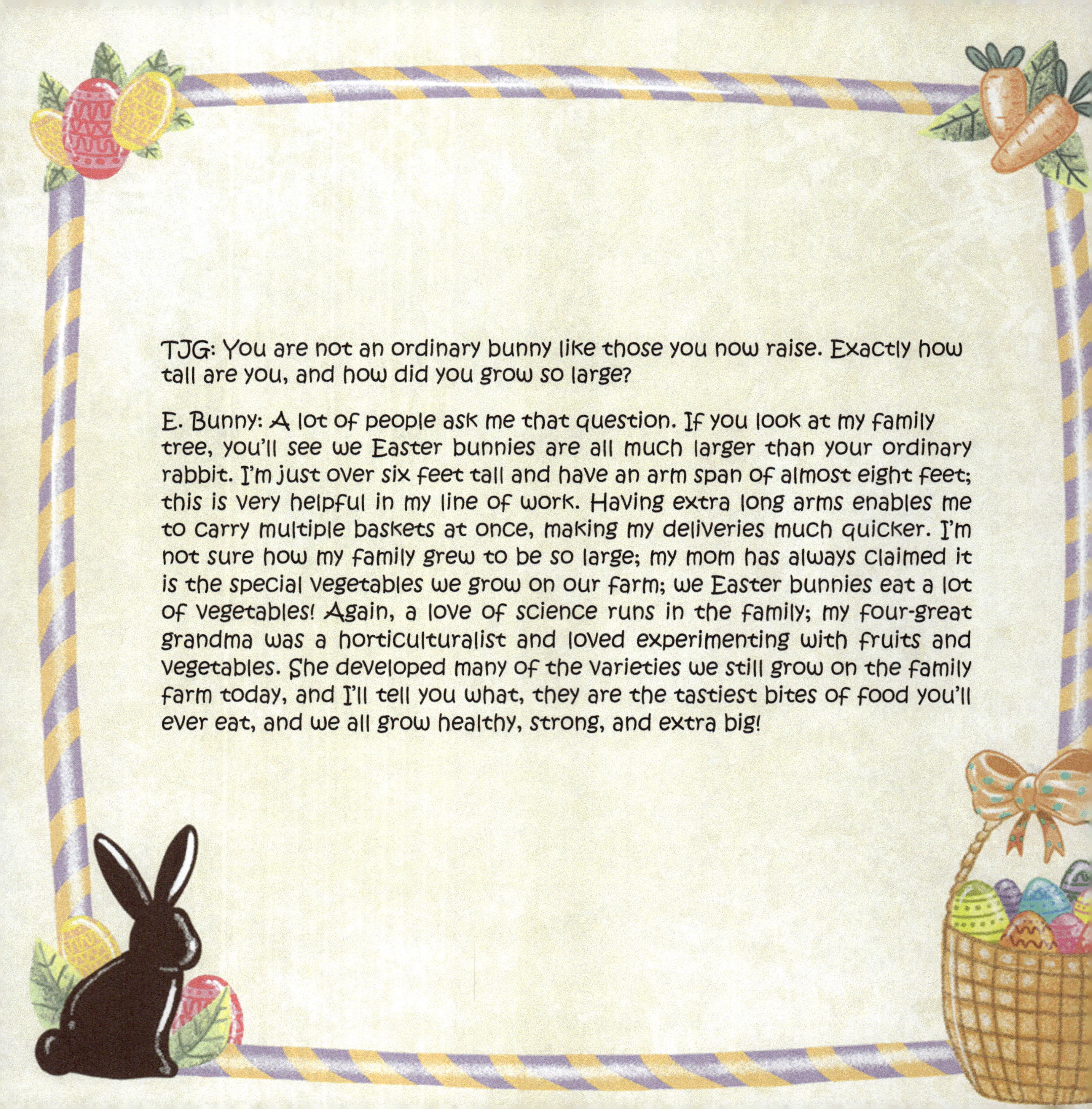

TJG: You are not an ordinary bunny like those you now raise. Exactly how tall are you, and how did you grow so large?

E. Bunny: A lot of people ask me that question. If you look at my family tree, you'll see we Easter bunnies are all much larger than your ordinary rabbit. I'm just over six feet tall and have an arm span of almost eight feet; this is very helpful in my line of work. Having extra long arms enables me to carry multiple baskets at once, making my deliveries much quicker. I'm not sure how my family grew to be so large; my mom has always claimed it is the special vegetables we grow on our farm; we Easter bunnies eat a lot of vegetables! Again, a love of science runs in the family; my four-great grandma was a horticulturalist and loved experimenting with fruits and vegetables. She developed many of the varieties we still grow on the family farm today, and I'll tell you what, they are the tastiest bites of food you'll ever eat, and we all grow healthy, strong, and extra big!

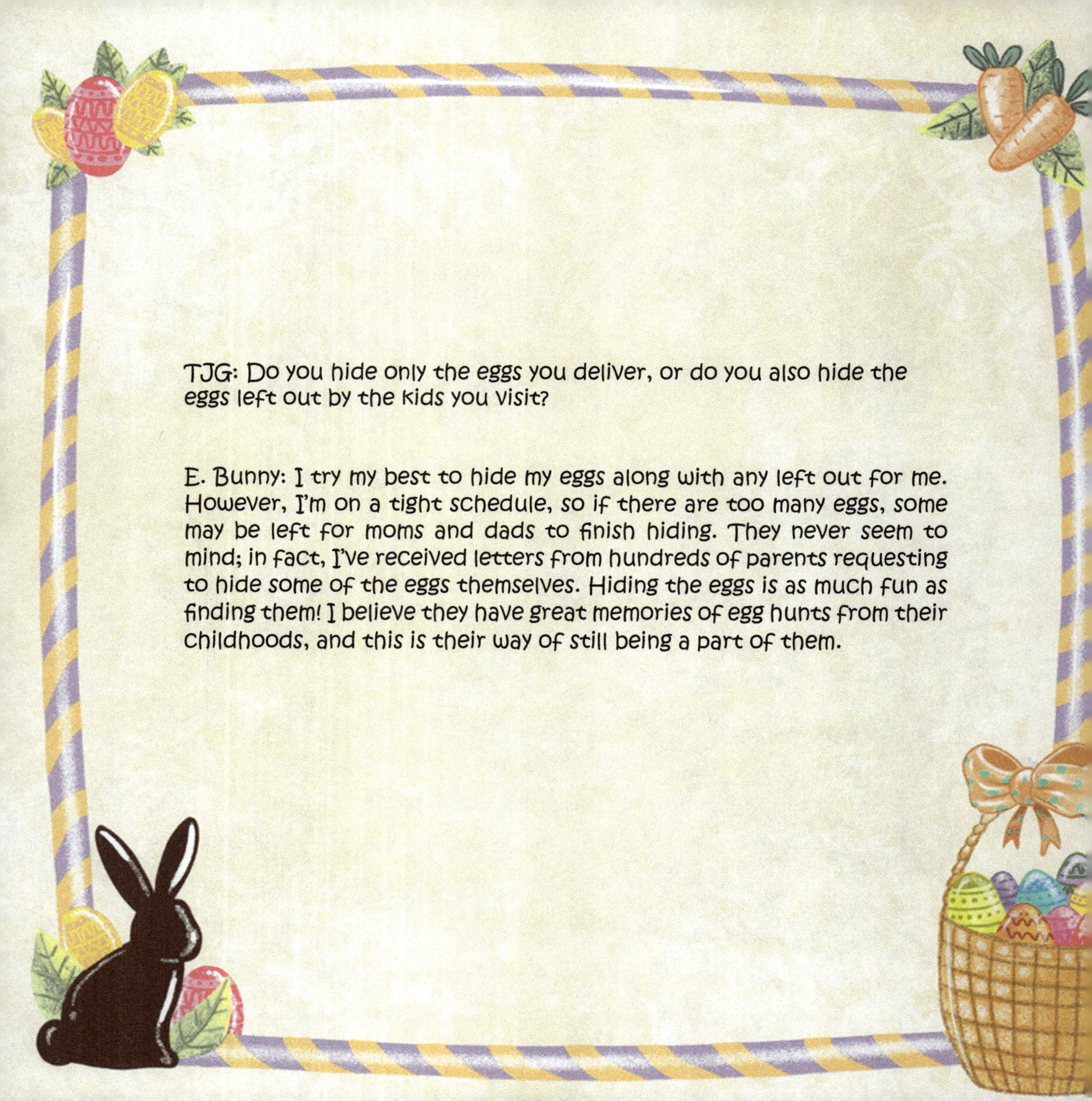

TJG: Do you hide only the eggs you deliver, or do you also hide the eggs left out by the kids you visit?

E. Bunny: I try my best to hide my eggs along with any left out for me. However, I'm on a tight schedule, so if there are too many eggs, some may be left for moms and dads to finish hiding. They never seem to mind; in fact, I've received letters from hundreds of parents requesting to hide some of the eggs themselves. Hiding the eggs is as much fun as finding them! I believe they have great memories of egg hunts from their childhoods, and this is their way of still being a part of them.

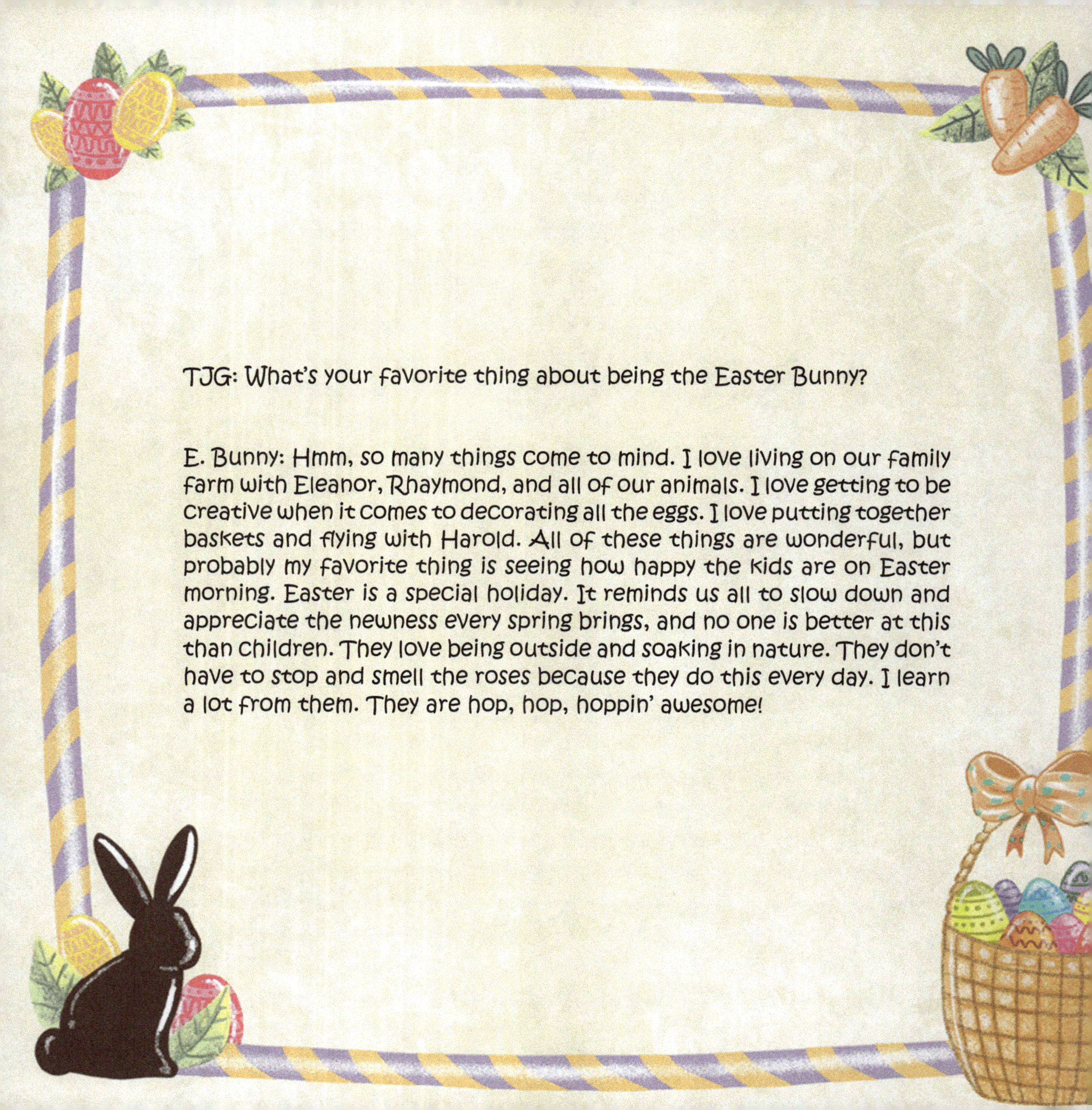

TJG: What's your favorite thing about being the Easter Bunny?

E. Bunny: Hmm, so many things come to mind. I love living on our family farm with Eleanor, Rhaymond, and all of our animals. I love getting to be creative when it comes to decorating all the eggs. I love putting together baskets and flying with Harold. All of these things are wonderful, but probably my favorite thing is seeing how happy the kids are on Easter morning. Easter is a special holiday. It reminds us all to slow down and appreciate the newness every spring brings, and no one is better at this than children. They love being outside and soaking in nature. They don't have to stop and smell the roses because they do this every day. I learn a lot from them. They are hop, hop, hoppin' awesome!

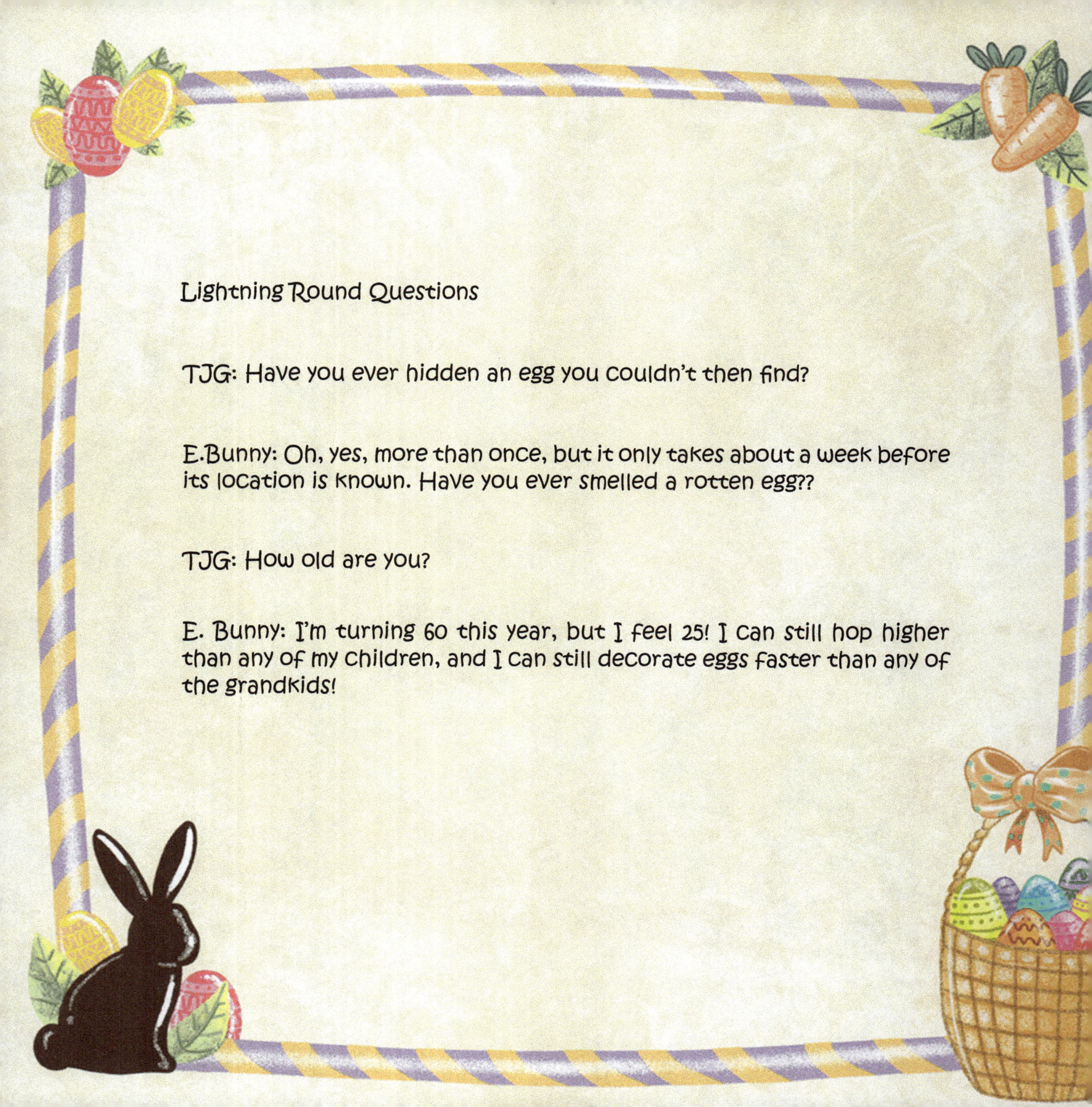

Lightning Round Questions

TJG: Have you ever hidden an egg you couldn't then find?

E.Bunny: Oh, yes, more than once, but it only takes about a week before its location is known. Have you ever smelled a rotten egg??

TJG: How old are you?

E. Bunny: I'm turning 60 this year, but I feel 25! I can still hop higher than any of my children, and I can still decorate eggs faster than any of the grandkids!

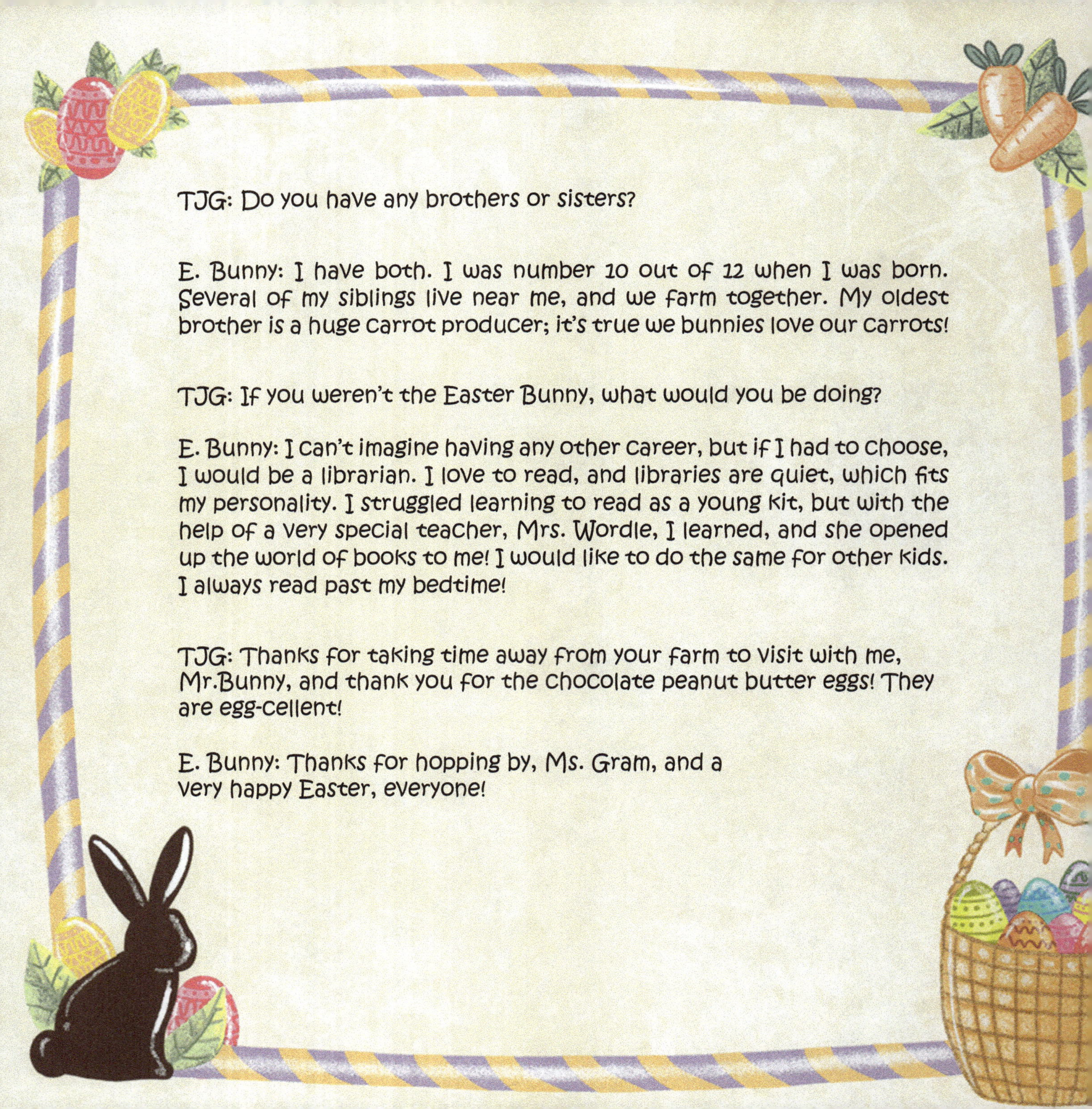

TJG: Do you have any brothers or sisters?

E. Bunny: I have both. I was number 10 out of 12 when I was born. Several of my siblings live near me, and we farm together. My oldest brother is a huge carrot producer; it's true we bunnies love our carrots!

TJG: If you weren't the Easter Bunny, what would you be doing?

E. Bunny: I can't imagine having any other career, but if I had to choose, I would be a librarian. I love to read, and libraries are quiet, which fits my personality. I struggled learning to read as a young kit, but with the help of a very special teacher, Mrs. Wordle, I learned, and she opened up the world of books to me! I would like to do the same for other kids. I always read past my bedtime!

TJG: Thanks for taking time away from your farm to visit with me, Mr.Bunny, and thank you for the chocolate peanut butter eggs! They are egg-cellent!

E. Bunny: Thanks for hopping by, Ms. Gram, and a very happy Easter, everyone!

SKATEBOARD
SECRETS

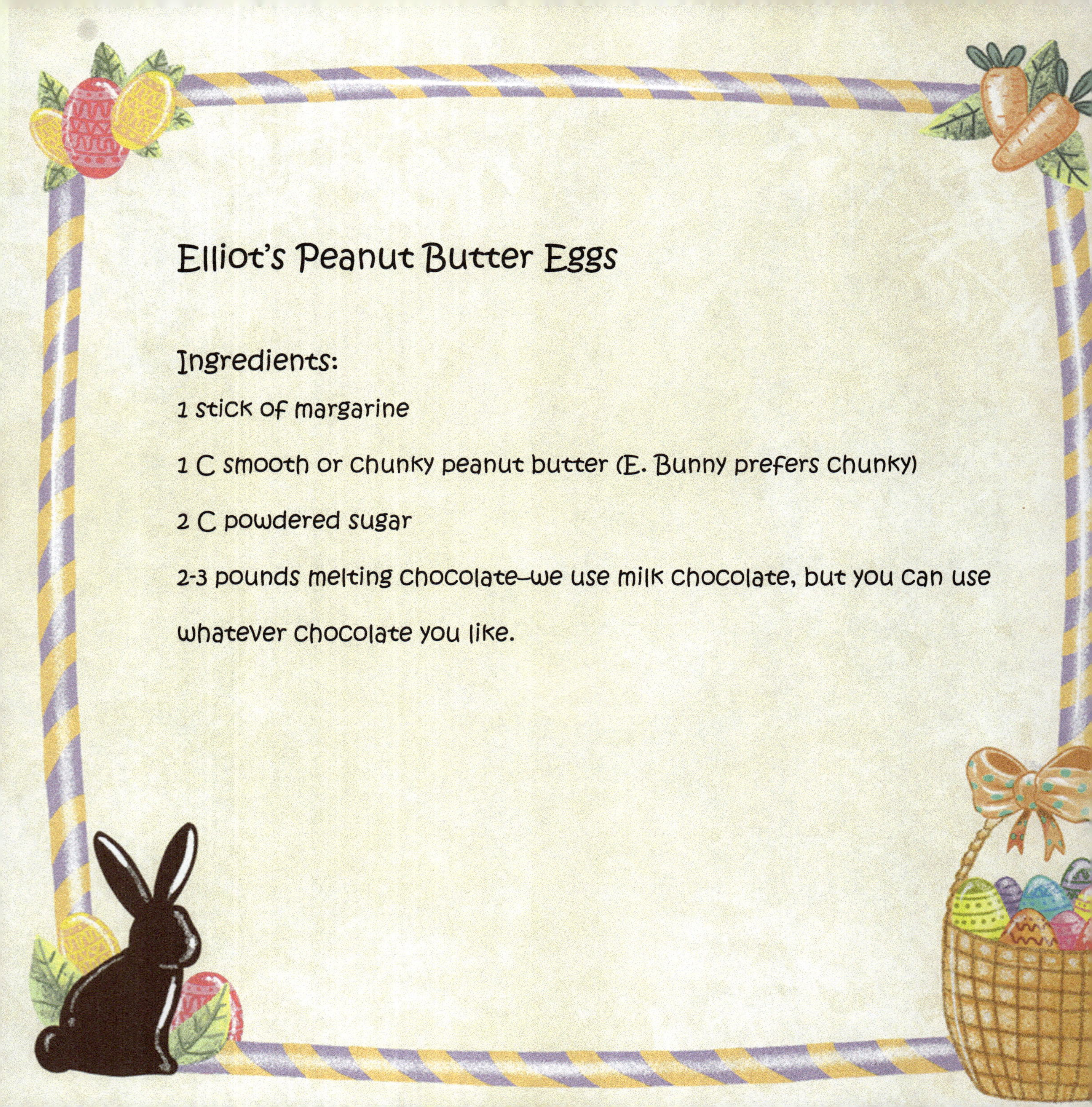

Elliot's Peanut Butter Eggs

Ingredients:

1 stick of margarine

1 C smooth or chunky peanut butter (E. Bunny prefers chunky)

2 C powdered sugar

2-3 pounds melting chocolate—we use milk chocolate, but you can use

whatever chocolate you like.

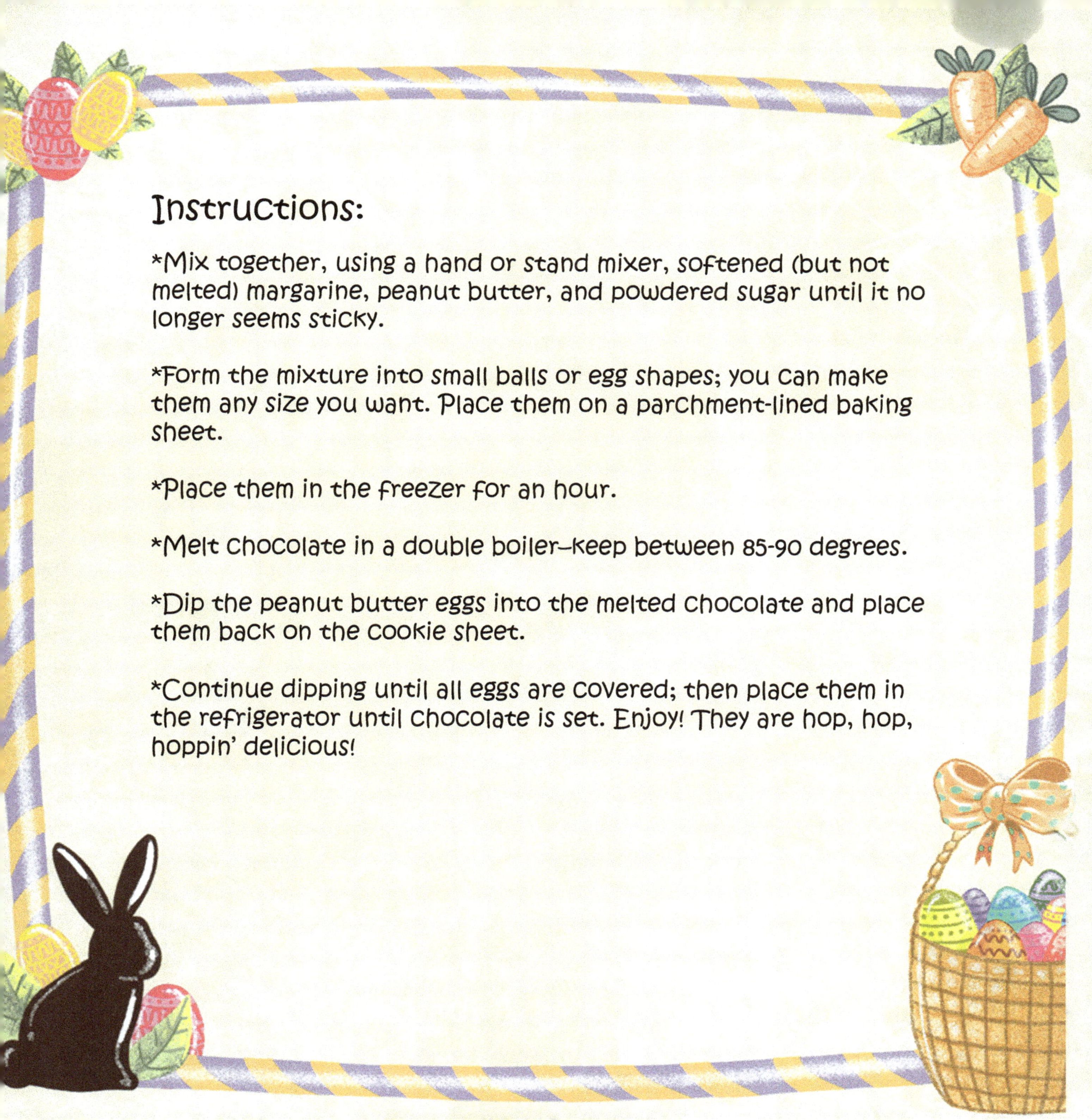

Instructions:

*Mix together, using a hand or stand mixer, softened (but not melted) margarine, peanut butter, and powdered sugar until it no longer seems sticky.

*Form the mixture into small balls or egg shapes; you can make them any size you want. Place them on a parchment-lined baking sheet.

*Place them in the freezer for an hour.

*Melt chocolate in a double boiler—keep between 85-90 degrees.

*Dip the peanut butter eggs into the melted chocolate and place them back on the cookie sheet.

*Continue dipping until all eggs are covered; then place them in the refrigerator until chocolate is set. Enjoy! They are hop, hop, hoppin' delicious!